For Beau — J.O.
For Clara x — L.G.

OXFORD
UNIVERSITY PRESS

Great Clarendon Street, Oxford OX2 6DP

Oxford University Press is a department of the University of Oxford.
It furthers the University's objective of excellence in research, scholarship,
and education by publishing worldwide in

Oxford   New York

Auckland   Cape Town   Dar es Salaam   Hong Kong   Karachi
Kuala Lumpur   Madrid   Melbourne   Mexico City   Nairobi
New Delhi   Shanghai   Taipei   Toronto

With offices in

Argentina   Austria   Brazil   Chile   Czech Republic   France   Greece
Guatemala   Hungary   Italy   Japan   Poland   Portugal   Singapore
South Korea   Switzerland   Thailand   Turkey   Ukraine   Vietnam

Oxford is a registered trade mark of Oxford University Press
in the UK and in certain other countries

Text © Jan Ormerod 2011
Illustrations © Lindsey Gardiner 2011

The moral rights of the author and illustrator have been asserted
Database right Oxford University Press (maker)

First published in 2011

British Library Cataloguing in Publication

Data available

ISBN: 978-0-19-278014-0 (Hardback)
ISBN: 978-0-19-278016-4 (Paperback with audio CD)
ISBN: 978-0-19-278015-7 (Paperback)

1 3 5 7 9 10 8 6 4 2

Printed in China

Paper used in the production of this book is a natural,
recyclable product made from wood grown in sustainable forests.
The manufacturing process conforms to the environmental
regulations of the country of origin

The Animal Bop Won't STOP!

Jan
Ormerod

Lindsey
Gardiner

OXFORD
UNIVERSITY PRESS

The animal bop just won't stop, so move your body from **bottom** to **top**!

Wiggle your hips,
let your
arms float free,

wibbly jellyfish under the sea!

Meerkat,

meerkat,

stand up

tall,

brrr, brrr, brrr,

it's a warning call,

run and hide!

Lambs go jumping just for fun,

so skippety, hoppity, everyone.

Like a prowling lion softly c r e e p,

be a growling lion . . .

make a great

Hibberty,
hobberty,
blobble-obble-obble,

wobble your head, do the turkey gobble!

The loris is truly, really slooooow . . .

see how slooooooowly you can go.

Stick out your tongue, stretch up

to the sky, chew like **giraffe**, way **up** high.

It's zany,
it's zippy,
it's the pony trot,

knees up,

toes down,

dance on the spot.

Strut along like a bold black crow,

with a Caw-Caw, Caw-Caw

as you go.

Flounce and flutter,

screech out loud,

swish and sashay

with the peacock crowd.

Curl up with koala,
shut your eyes tight,
quiet in the gum tree
all through the night...